James Linen

The Later Poems and Songs of James Linen

James Linen

The Later Poems and Songs of James Linen

ISBN/EAN: 9783744773904

Printed in Europe, USA, Canada, Australia, Japan

Cover: Foto ©Andreas Hilbeck / pixelio.de

More available books at **www.hansebooks.com**

THE LATER

POEMS AND SONGS

OF

JAMES LINEN.

WRITTEN BETWEEN THE YEARS 1865 AND 1873.

"Peace! Independence! Truth! go forth
Earth's compass round;
And your high-priesthood shall make earth
All hallowed ground."

THOMAS CAMPBELL.

New York:
W. J. WIDDLETON, PUBLISHER,

SAN FRANCISCO:
A. ROMAN & COMPANY.

1873.

JOHN ROSS & CO., PRINTERS, 27 ROSE STREET, NEW YORK.

TO

William Cullen Bryant, Esq.

During the long period of nearly forty years, I have received from you many kind favors of a social and literary character. You smiled approvingly on my earliest poetic efforts. Having the same veneration for your exalted worth as a man, with an undiminished admiration for your ability as a poet, as I entertained when a youth, to whom could I inscribe this production with so much grateful propriety as to yourself? My larger volumes were dedicated to you, and, with your permission, I lay down respectfully at the shrine of your genius this little offering of my humble Muse.

Cordially your friend,

JAMES LINEN.

THE present volume requires no apology for its publication. Some of the poems and songs have been popular and drifting about, and appearing occasionally without even the author's name. Having sufficient material on hand, I concluded to publish them under my own supervision. Eight years ago, I gave to the world my miscellaneous writings in prose and verse, which were well received at the time. I have since published "The Golden Gate," with illustrations and historical notes.

Some of the lyrics have been so popular that they have been set to music both at home and abroad. Such compositions will be found in the pages of this volume, arranged side by side, with similar effusions of a later date. I hope it will please my friends to see them published uniformly and together.

My Muse feels none of the infirmities peculiar to old age. She is still vigorous, and in the full enjoyment of mental health. However, she prefers repose to the labor of toiling for an empty name. For many years, she has been kindly fostered by a generous Press. Henceforth she will seek the social sweets of retirement. Her task is done, and her ambition has been abundantly gratified. The companion and sweet solace of my life now bows herself graciously out of the Republic of Letters.

NEW YORK, July 4, 1872.

CONTENTS.

———◆———

POEMS.

SONGS.

EPITAPHS AND EPIGRAMS.

POEMS.

THE POET'S MISSION.

BENEATH the poet's wandering feet fair flowers for ever
   spring,
And o'er the poet's thoughtful head sweet birds for ever sing :
He tunes his harp to stirring strains, in all things beauty sees,
And music weird and wild he hears in every whistling breeze.

Though wrestling with his passions strong, his thoughts soar
   upward still
To spheres beyond all human ken, where fancy roams at will ;
His keen eye scans creation o'er, and finds a peaceful home
In every star that glitters bright in yonder sapphire dome.

With flowers he decks the arid waste, and drinks from desert
   springs,
And o'er the face of nature rude a robe of beauty flings ;
He worships on the mountain-tops, and, kneeling on the sod,
With hands upraised, all prophet-like, he communes with his
   God.

2

He frowns on kings and hireling tools who smile at guilty
 Wrong ;
He holds up high to public scorn proud knaves in deathless
 song ;
And while he pleads in earnest tones for honors to the
 brave,
His burning words strong fetters melt that bind the bleeding
 slave.

Dark clouds, with living lightning charged, across the sky
 may roll,
And thunders shake with trembling fears the world from
 Pole to Pole ;
But he who thrills the human heart, the gifted son of Time,
Stands forth amid the tempest wild, and paints the scene
 sublime.

From Truth the poet never swerves, and firm by Freedom
 stands,
And scorns the shield of tyrant flags in dark, down-trodden
 lands ;
But while he humbly worships God, and bows to laws divine,
He tears the mask from canting priests who kneel at Error's
 shrine.

While Reason stands in boundless wastes, bewildered, lost,
 and dumb,
Swift to the bard's conceptive mind bright visions trooping
 come ;

He wanders through the orbs of space, sees worlds on worlds
    arise,
Where dimly Faith in silence points to realms that Doubt
    denies.

His kingdom is the human heart, in which he rears his
    throne ;
His subjects are the passions wild that due allegiance own.
No monarch that holds regal sway, and wears a jewelled
    crown,
Can ever crush the poet's rule, or drag his empire down.

The Bunch of Heather Bells.

AS on thy stem a thousand bells
     In fragrant beauty hing,
So, round my auld time-withered heart
     Sweet recollections cling.
Thy bells to me have tuneful tongues
     That ring auld Scotia's praise,
And hallow'd thochts come rushing back
     To scenes o' bygane days.

Ere thorns o' care grew in my heart,
     I lap ower mossy dykes,
Whaur heather linties sing their sangs,
     And bumbees build their bykes.
I've wandered ower the weary waste,
     And seen it wrapt in snaw,
Heard lammies bleat on purple moors
     Whaur scented breezes blaw.

O bonnie bunch o' blooming bells!
     My heart wi' rapture thrills,
While thus I hail thee as a friend
     Fresh frae my native hills.

Thou'rt red and strong wi' moorland health,
  And, when compared wi' thee,
The painted flowers o' tropic lands
  Are sickly things to me.

O golden days o' joyous youth !
  What transports sweet are mine,
When mem'ry thro' the mists o' years
  Glints back on auld langsyne.
Oh ! for ae blink o' Scotia's glens,
  Her mountains wild and bare !
Bound by the ties time canna break,
  My heart still lingers there.

ƒONSCIENCE.

"Whatever creed be taught, or land be trod,
Man's conscience is the oracle of God."
BYRON.

TELL me, O Conscience! what thou art,
That fires the brain, and wrings the heart;
That haunts the guilty mind with fears,
And fills the eyes with bitter tears;
That keeps the memory on the rack,
By bringing recollections back;
That plays with feelings at thy will,
And tortures with consummate skill;
Whose task it is, by smile or frown,
To lift man up, or drag him down;
Whose stings are keener far than steel
Which felons in dark dungeons feel.
The prince may golden favors shower,
Yet he is subject to thy power;
The priest may preach some creed of gloom,
And sing of bliss beyond the tomb;
But thou canst read his thought profound,
Lone Sentinel of sacred ground!

The hero honor's path may tread,
And his great name world-wide be spread ;
But glory brings not peace of mind—
That jewel rare, so hard to find.
From thy dominion none can flee,
For mortals all must bow to thee !
Tell me, O Conscience ! what thou art,
Weird watchman of the human heart !

Art thou the child of wretched Care,
That murders Sleep, and mocks Despair ;
That fills with pangs the human breast,
And robs the guilty head of rest ;
That mutely weeps o'er crimes untold,
Where Vice buys Virtue with its gold ;
Whose records by some mystic hand
Are written in a fadeless land ?
Tell me, O Conscience ! what thou art,
Weird watchman of the human heart !

The soul, that claims celestial birth,
Finds naught but tainted joys on earth ;
Imprisoned in a cell of clay
That yields to laws of swift decay—
Too pure for such a horrid hell,
Where shapeless fiends in anguish dwell—
The spirit-tenant of the heart
Is ever yearning to depart ;
Like some caged warbler, to be free,
That it may soar, O God, to thee !

O Conscience! mute, mysterious guest!
Man fain would pluck thee from his breast,
As if thou wert his deadly foe,
The only cause of human woe;
Could he but snatch thy golden crown,
And madly pull thy temple down,
Dark Vice would rear her bloody shrines
Where perish hopes, and Virtue pines;
Strike but the brave heart-monarch dumb,
And earth a desert would become.

When man can feel a conscience clear,
What wrongs and dangers need he fear?
Calmly at his departing breath
It takes away the stings from death:
It nobly braves the coward world,
Till Reason from her throne be hurled:
With all the feelings of the heart
It gently plays a leading part,
In concert acting with the soul
When passions wild brook no control;
Close by life's purple fountain found,
It guards the spot as holy ground.
Tell me, O Conscience! what thou art,
Weird watchman of the human heart!

Y I R T U E .

O WOMAN ! what a wretch thou art,
　　If virtue reigns not in thy heart !
By some kind Providence designed
To comfort and to bless mankind ;
Like some sweet angel from above,
To cheer the fireside with thy love,
And make thy home a home of peace,
Where joys connubial never cease ;
Where looks and honeyed words are kind,
And tender ties affections bind—
Who dare invade such hallowed ground,
Where no dark passions lurk around ?

Oft beauty Virtue's claims neglect,
Who courts not, but commands respect ;
Cased in an armor that's divine,
She, sleepless, guards her sacred shrine,
And shuns the gilded halls of vice,
Where bastard virtue hath its price ;
Despising Mammon's purse-proud slaves,
She spurns the proffered gold of knaves ;

Her heart from all deceit is free,
And looks for strength, O God, to thee!
She may be poor, but still her name
Untarnished is by deeds of shame;
She may be clothed in rags and need,
In touching tones with pity plead;
Yet, conscious that she's pure and just,
She keeps secure her priceless trust.

While others quaff libations up,
She spurns the dangers of the cup,
And proudly, with imperious frown,
She casts the tempting goblet down;
Her sober reason, strong and pure,
Knows reeling thrones are insecure.
So, sparkling wine may fire the brain,
And lead to years of bitter pain.
The scornful flashing of her eye
All crafty snares of art defy;
From her one keen, indignant glance
Forbids a villain to advance;
Confused, he seeks a swift retreat,
Or kneels a craven at her feet;
She towers above all vice and shame,
And glories in her stainless name.

When Honor comes with motive pure,
The welcome is made sweetly sure;

Her modest and her simple air,
And blushes on her cheeks so fair ;
The music of her guileless tongue,
That never worth and merit stung ;
The curtains that so mildly rise,
And graceful hang o'er wistful eyes ;
The gentle heaving of the breast,
Where all the passions calmly rest,
Present a bride so true and warm
That shafts of envy fail to harm ;
Her loving heart, when fairly won,
The brightest jewel 'neath the sun,
Confiding in her chosen spouse,
Keeps sacred all her bridal vows.

TIME.

THROUGH mists that hang over the Past,
    No mortal his story can trace;
He sits on a mystical throne,
    The first and the last of his race.

No jewels shine bright on his crown,
    And mutely he reigns as of old;
His archives by angels are kept,
    Which no human eye can behold.

When Earth was a planet of fire,
    In wonder he rode on the storm,
And gazed at the red, flaming ball,
    Ere matter was moulded to form.

Amid the dread deluge of fire,
    He saw the huge mountains arise,
Until their bleak summits were lost
    In the white-rolling clouds of the skies.

When Nature was writhing in pain,
  And struggling as if to be free,
He saw roaring billows shrink back,
  And islands leap out of the sea.

When flames their wild fury had spent,
  And left bare the crust of the globe,
He saw smiling Nature look glad,
  And graced with an emerald robe.

From chaos he saw beauty spring,
  And order march forth in its train ;
But to find out the date of his birth,
  Man's efforts are futile and vain.

The keen eye of man fails to pierce
  The pall and the blackness of night,
And Science gets 'wildered and lost
  In search of the truth-guiding light.

The Scholar may boast of his lore,
  The Sophist and wrangler may rave ;
But rocks and volcanoes are dumb,
  And fossils are mute as the grave.

Old Time has seen symbols, and creeds,
  And races of men swept away ;
While the earth was smoking with blood,
  And strewn with the wrecks of decay.

Let builders build temples of stone,
　Bound strongly with iron and brass;
Their years may be thousands, yet they
　Shall into forgetfulness pass.

The sage may be led by the truth—
　The light only known to the few;
But no seer the veil can withdraw
　That hides the dark future from view.

D E C A Y .

SHE sits like an old withered hag
   By a shrine all broken and gray;
The owls give her music at night,
   And lizards amuse her by day.

She loves amid ruins to muse,
   Where no one disturbs her retreat;
The wrecks of old altars and thrones
   Lie scattered around at her feet.

She treads on green carpets of moss,
   Spread on aisles where beauty once trod,
And stares at grand arches that rung
   With anthems and praises to God.

The worms have drilled holes in the doors,
   Whose hinges are covered with rust;
And turrets and towers lose their strength,
   And topple fast down to the dust.

The bells that were noisy are mute,
   And niches where images stood
Are haunts of the night-bird, and where
   The bats nurse their ravenous brood.

Through windows of Gothic design,
   Hung round with green ivy festoons,
Through columns the pride of the Past,
   The wild and weird winds whistle tunes.

She reigns in the palace and cot;
   Art shrinks from her life-wasting breath,
And old Time declares her to be
   The haggard twin-sister of Death.

She blights the fair rose on the cheek,
   And tames the wild passions of lust;
The flesh leaves the bones at her touch,
   And the bones are soon powdered to dust.

Her eyes are deep-sunken and dim,
   Her hollow cheeks withered and wan:
And, wrapped in a mystical cloak,
   She grins with contempt upon man.

Her march is triumphant and slow,
   With no flaunting banners unfurled:
No mortal can tell where she lives,
   Or how she came into the world.

Her laws are not subject to change,
  Nor can she be purchased with gold ;
And, till the last trumpet shall sound,
  Her story can never be told.

βYGANE ᴅAYS.

'TIS sweet to muse on bygane days,
  When, under gentle rule,
With no care in my thoughtless head,
  I toddled aff to schule.
The skylark sung his morning lays
  Up o'er the daisied lea,
And music gushed in melting strains
  Frae ilka bush and tree.

The hawthorn wi' its blossoms white,
  The gowans at my feet,
And clover red in fragrant fields
  Sent forth their odors sweet ;
The wild rose on my pathway bloomed,
  The flower was on the pea,
And heather-bells and gowden broom
  Gave honey to the bee.

I've wandered ower the mosses, where
  The moorland lintie sings,

And butterflies on blossoms fair
  Fold up their painted wings ;
I've gathered slaes and berries wild
  On hills that rung wi' glee,
And aft to pu' the crimson fruit
  I climbed the rowan tree.

I've wandered ower the battle-fields
  That mighty men have trod,
Seen sacred spots where marshalled troops
  Sung praises to their God ;
I've stood upon the hallowed ground
  Where Bruce his flag unfurled,
And, by one bold and daring stroke,
  Gave freedom to the world.

These were the bright and sunny days
  Of life's sweet budding spring,
Before I felt that manhood's years
  Sad cares and sorrows bring.
Time, in his weary onward flight,
  Hath wings that never tire ;
But age, way-worn, sinks slowly down,
  Outliving passion's fire.

O Scotia ! Freedom's chosen land,
  Thou still art dear to me ;
In age, the same as early youth,
  My heart still clings to thee !

Thy rugged glens and fertile dales,
Thy mountains wild and grand,
Spring up in fancy's pleasant dreams,
Like some enchanted land.

GREENWOOD.

THE lone stranger enters a Gothic gate,
  And he mutely wanders around,
While the sculptured tombs in their silence tell
  That he treads upon holy ground.

He listens, and hears such a dirge-like sound,
  And he wonders what it can be;
For 'tis not the wail of a broken heart,
  Nor the wail of the surging sea.

As the sleepers hear not the dismal tones,
  Let the storm and the tempest rave;
For what reck the dead for the wild, weird winds
  That break not the peace of the grave?

From their toils and cares here the weary sleep
  On a couch that is damp and cold;
And kindly the green turf hides from the sight
  The mute forms of the young and old.

Here lies pampered wealth with a tombstone fame
  That once knelt to a golden god;
And here merit rests from an active life,
  Covered up by the grassy sod.

When the purple stream of the human heart
  No longer from its fountain flows,
In Death's freezing arms, where no troubles lurk,
  Here the rich and the poor repose.

Let defiant pride bend its haughty head,
  And hear the sermons dead men preach ;
It will humbled be, and deep lessons learn
  Which pulpit lore can never teach.

In the winding paths and the fragrant groves.
  Where graceful art with nature vies,
And covered with flowers that in beauty bloom,
  Death coldly sleeps in sweet disguise.

Sir Walter Scott's Monument

IN CENTRAL PARK.

WHILE to Scott we fondly cling,
    Sweetest bards his praises sing ;
And the glens and mountains ring
    With stirring strains of melody :

Let them bend their heads in shame
Who would blot his glorious name,
Blazing on the scroll of fame
    In fadeless lustre brilliantly.

With a smile the just may wear,
'Neath a crushing load of care
Such as mortals seldom bear,
    He bore his cross triumphantly.

God, who sends the grateful shower
To revive the drooping flower,
Gave him grand creative power—
    The rare gift of divinity.

Let no eyes with tears be wet,
Heave no sighs of deep regret,
For his death he bravely met—
    The fate of all humanity.

In his name the virtues blend,
Honor was his steadfast friend,
Faith sustained him to the end
    With hopes of immortality.

Where his ashes now repose,
Swift the Tweed in beauty flows;
And the weary pilgrim goes
    To pay his homage silently.

Glory with a ringing sound
Spreads his name the world around,
Who made Scotland classic ground,
    And sung her praise exultingly.

O'er the mountain and the dell
He could throw a wizard spell,
And some thrilling story tell
    In tones of deathless minstrelsy.

In the world of mighty mind,
His great name will live enshrined,
And shall warm admirers find
    In a remote posterity.

In his statue art can trace
Features of his manly face,
Wanting only living grace
 To give the form mortality.

As his fame will never die,
May his statue, firm and high,
While the storms of time sweep by,
 Brave all their might defiantly.

The Sparrows.

WHEN wintry winds blow bleak and keen, and snow-
flakes thickly fall,
Oh! hear ye not amid the storm the starving sparrows'
call?
Then, while your hearts with kindness swell, give succor
to the poor,
And ne'er forget the chirping birds that hop around your
door.

They leave their footprints in the snow, and perch on leaf-
less trees,
Where, cold and numb, the little things sit trembling in
the breeze;
They are for some wise purpose sent, and play their humble part,
And seem familiar with the chords that thrill the human
heart.

They nestle in some ivied wall, some crevice in the eaves,
And rest their little naked feet in nests of withered leaves;

Oft hands of charity build cots, where snug their feathered
forms
Are safe from winter's biting frosts and from the midnight
storms.

They seem to know the friendly door, by pinching hunger led;
And who would wrong the harmless race that are by mercy
fed ?
Oh ! while they crave the simple crumbs that from your table
fall,
Let plenty give and warm hearts beat responsive to their call.

Soon nature from a torpid state to life anew will spring,
And vernal winds will softly blow, and woodlands sweetly
ring ;
The sparrows have no gift of song, yet, though their tongues
be dumb,
Their little breasts will throb with joy when buds and blossoms come.

O ye who kneel at Mercy's throne ! if mercy you would find,
Drive not the beggar from your door, and to the birds be
kind ;
There is a Providence divine, and God, who rules o'er all,
Supplies the craving wants of man, and "marks the sparrow's
fall."

My Beloved Son.

WRITTEN FOR A BEREAVED MOTHER.

MY heart is wrung with bitter grief,
  And hopes are lowly laid;
For coldly sleeps my darling boy
  In Greenwood's leafy shade.

When but an infant on my knee,
  How witchingly he smiled!
And with his sweet and rosy face
  The weary hours beguiled.

None like a mother e'er can feel,
  Or can her sorrows share;
The burden that weighs down the soul
  Alone she has to bear.

Methinks I see his curly locks,
  His little manly brow;
And, oh! I'd give a thousand worlds,
  Could I but kiss him now.

My broken heart would leap with joy,
 No more be wrung with pain,
Could I but snatch him from the grave,
 And bring him back again.

But why muse on such idle dreams,
 On things that ne'er can be?
Yet while I live, departed son,
 My thoughts will be of thee!

There is a hope to which I cling—
 That, in a realm of joy,
We'll meet again to part no more,
 My dear, beloved boy!

├INES TO AN ρLD ┬OOTH.

FAITHFUL, bygone masticator !
    Though not a thing of beauty,
For threescore long and weary years
    Thou hast performed thy duty.
Reluctantly we part, old friend !
    Hadst thou been rooted stronger,
I have no doubt but at thy post
    Thou wouldst have lingered longer.

Mute relic of a grinding race,
    That once shone bright and pearly,
So firmly set in coral gums
    Beside thy comrades early,
Thou art a brave part of myself—
    The aider of digestion ;
In crushing piles to shapeless hash,
    None dared thy skill to question.

The hardest nuts that ever grew
    Tried oft thy stubborn mettle ;
But, like all other things, they failed
    Thy firmness to unsettle.

As grim Decay did not succeed
  In piercing thee with drilling,
Thou hadst no caverns deep and dark
  Requiring dental filling.

Thy setting grew so old and void
  Of sympathetic feeling,
It shrunk and left thee standing bare,
  Like some poor drunkard reeling.
O life-long friend ! for ever proud
  Of thy time-honored calling,
Thy kindred organs feel the loss
  Of thy untimely falling.

With fever hot the head might reel,
  And hands might be unsteady ;
But, true to thy allotted task,
  Thou wert for ever ready—
A slave to my capricious will,
  A chattel, dumb and senseless,
That stood so long in danger's ranks,
  A hero all defenceless.

The tongue, which antedates thy birth,
  Thy busy, chatty neighbor,
It claims to be to some extent
  Partaker of thy labor.
Amongst all other mortal friends,
  None to thy end stood nearer,

And, trusting in thy certain aid,
 It spoke in accents clearer.

Companion of my wayward life,
 In travels far and pleasant,
Through tropic climes and regions bleak.
 Thou wert for ever present.
Long carried proudly in my mouth,
 Now resting in my pocket,
Thou hast no heir to fill thy place.
 Thy lone, deserted socket.

Thy fellows may to Greenwood go,
 With hearse-plumes waving o'er them.
And in the grave unheeded lie,
 Like millions gone before them ;
But as for thee, poor lifeless thing,
 Sans tale of shame or glory,
I'll keep thee amongst fossils rare
 As a *memento mori.*

THE CENTENARIAN.

I AM dreary and chill, I am feeble and old,
  And the life-giving rays of the warm sun are cold;
From the keen frosts of age to what land can I flee?
What is summer to youth is bleak winter to me.

For what object I'm spared, for what purpose I live,
Human wisdom is dumb, and no reason can give;
I have nothing to love, I have nothing to crave,
And life's sun will soon set in the night of the grave.

All my fond-cherished schemes like sweet visions have fled,
And the friends of my youth and my kindred are dead;
I am deaf as a rock that is dashed by the sea,
And am withered and gnarled like an old sapless tree.

Naught can gladden my heart—I am weary of strife,
And can struggle no more in the battle of life;
As my trust is in God, so I fear not my end,
And I know, when Death comes, he will come as a friend.

As I sit by the door, lone and desolate now,
Where the winds kindly fan my old time-wrinkled brow,
I oft dream of the past with eyes brimming with tears,
And a mind that gets lost in the dark mists of years.

Oh! I once had a wife—dear companion to me!
She was gentle and sweet as a mortal can be;
Soon she languished and died, and at one fatal blow
All my hopes and my peace in her grave were laid low.

For a season too brief with a child I was blest:
With her mother she lies, where the world-weary rest;
And they sleep in one grave 'neath a green willow-tree,
Where the birds sweetly sing, though they sing not for me.

Age has bleached my hair white, and so dim is my sight
That clear noon I scarce know from the darkness of night;
With a feeble, bent form, a heart crushed with despair,
The sad burden of life is too heavy to bear.

The cold creeps up my limbs, and the red stream grows chill;
Soon the fountain will freeze, and for ever be still;
Though my body is weak, I am strong in my faith,
And long to pass through the dark shadows of death.

To my Daughter Josephine.

O PART of my being! so loving and free,
  In joy or in sorrow, my dreams are of thee!
In each kindred feature, in each striking line,
I see my own image traced nicely in thine.

When lonely and weary I think of the past,
And glance at the future with shadows o'ercast,
Oh! quick as the moments that rapidly flee
Revert my sad musings, sweet daughter, to thee!

Through all trying changes, be happy as now,
With no clouds of sorrow o'erhanging thy brow;
What rude hand so daring as seek to displace
The bright sunny gladness that beams on thy face?

Be peaceful thy slumbers, unshadowed thy way,
And time spare thy beauty from speedy decay;
And, oh! my fair daughter, so gentle and kind,
May life's heavy burden rest light on thy mind.

Where'er thou mayst wander, my hope and my pride,
May faith be thy comfort, and virtue thy guide ;
Thy heart, warm and tender, by care never wrung,
Unwounded by envy, by malice unstung.

Shun snares in life's pathway that shine to allure
A peace that is holy, a heart that is pure ;
And when in thy chamber thou bendest the knee,
Remember thy father, who fondly loves thee !

Nil Desperandum.

O YE weary and brave! while ye battle with Care,
　Shut the door of the heart against haggard Despair;
For the tottering hopes upon which you have leaned
May be withered and crushed by the merciless fiend.

Though the clouds gather fast, and the light be withdrawn,
Soon the darkness will fade at the breaking of dawn,
And hopes that seem dead spring to beauty anew,
Like the sweet drooping flowers that are nursed by the dew.

Though the tempest be wild and the drifting bark frail,
And dark ruin and death seem to ride on the gale,
Soon the winds spend their strength, and tired waves fall
　　asleep,
And the soft zephyrs fan the calm face of the deep.

On the pathway of life, sad and gloomy appear
The dim shadows of grief and the phantoms of fear;
But when bright rays of hope the heart's deep chambers fill,
Lo! they vanish like mist from the brow of the hill.

There are losses we weep, there are crosses we bear,
And keen pangs that we feel that no mortal can share;
And oft wrongs in the heart are concealed and untold
Which pride hides from the world that is selfish and cold.

We may bask in fond smiles, we may gaze upon tears,
But the heart is unseen that is trembling with fears;
Who can coldly look on and see loved ones laid low,
And hopes scattered like leaves when the autumn winds blow ?

Until tears dim the eye and grief seams the fair brow,
Love may cherish a hope the tongue dare not avow;
In the breast that is true lurks no spirit of guile,
And the brave can lie down and meet death with a smile.

When Want enters the door, hollow friends may depart,
And no sunshine of joy cheer the desolate heart.
Let us bravely toil on; soon the light may appear
That will chase from the soul all the darkness of fear.

Buds and blossoms may fade, and sweet beauty may die,
While the living may weep or in sorrow may sigh;
Hope, still beaming with love when the spirit has fled,
Leaves a lingering smile on the face of the dead.

When the burden of life is too heavy to bear,
Let Faith live in the heart, and sweet Hope nestle there;
And the angel of death may soon usher you in
To a home that is pure and untainted by sin.

An Enigma.

——— — —

IN the depths of the sea, in the planets above,
　In the regions of woe, and the mansions of love,
There's a something that reigns and not subject to law—
Self-existent, a something that God never saw;
'Tis eternal like matter, and, knowing no birth,
It first saw beauty spring from the rugged, dull earth;
'Tis unerring in wisdom, untouched by decay,
Pervading all space with a limitless sway;
'Tis a something divine, and the stars of the night
Are the jewels that shine on its diadem bright;
So enshrined in a glory without stain or flaw,
Canst thou tell, then, O mortal! what God never saw?

Slaves of Fashion.

WHAT though their heads be dull as lead
   And thick as granite boulders,
Let ribbons flaunt like streamers gay
   Adown their necks and shoulders;
And let them go like saints to church,
   Sans brains with graceful carriage;
Their smiles, like snares, may catch the fools
   That laugh at vows of marriage.

Thus Fashion's slaves wed golden knaves
   That fill their homes with sorrow,
And solemn vows made fresh to-day
   Are broken on the morrow;
They see how loose are priestly knots,
   See hopes like blossoms wither,
And learn too late that love alone
   Can bind fond hearts together.

MAGGIE MITCHELL.

BONNIE Maggie, young and fair!
  Little fairy! jewel rare!
Virtue on her spotless throne
Proudly claims thee as her own,
And, to form thy sprightly mind,
All the graces have combined;
With thy witching charms of art
Thou canst thrill the human heart,
Tame the passions strong and wild,
Nature's sweet and wondrous child!

Bonnie Maggie, fair and young,
Be thou free from Slander's tongue;
Free from pain and free from sin,
Smiles without, and peace within;
Free from keen affliction's rod,
Cheered by hope with faith in God;
And, O Maggie! beauteous maid,
May thy laurels never fade,
Life be as a pleasant dream,
Gliding down time's rapid stream.

7

Fortune's child, though wealth be thine.
Never kneel at Mammon's shrine;
Where his slaves are firmly bound,
Withered hopes lie strewn around;
Men whose brows are seamed by care
Bend the knee and worship there;
If thou wouldst be truly blest,
Seek the peaceful shades of rest,
Where thy calm and cultured mind
Lasting joys may always find.

Who would wish to cling to earth?
Death is but a second birth:
Love and beauty ne'er decay
In the realm of endless day;
Through this vale of tears and strife
Mayst thou lead a happy life,
Longing for the golden prize
Wisely hid from mortal eyes;
Living with a stainless name,
Fadeless glory be thine aim.

Love and Revenge.

DEEP down in the heart glow the fires of hell,
　Where wild passions are wedded to fate,
And where slighted love pants for dark revenge,
　In a spirit of fiendish hate.
Honor feels the sting of a bitter wrong,
　And, with soul that is proud and brave,
It will cure its wounds in the blood of guilt,
　On the brink of a yawning grave.

Miles Standish.

IN days of old, Miles Standish preached
　Amid wild and barren rocks,
And Pilgrims grave with souls to save
　Heard his teachings orthodox.
Descendants of the *Mayflower* saints !
　Should you desire a teacher,
Join Fashion's train in Plymouth Church,
　And hear soul-saving Beecher.

Destiny.

IT has aye been the case, and it will be to the end,
   The tae half o' the warl kensna how the ither fend ;
Gif folk are unco poor, they're no fashed wi' muckle care—
A strong arm and licht heart can a weary burden bear.

Contentment is a bliss that the rich may never ken,
Frae some wee theekit cot hae aft sprung our muckle men ;
Tho' halls o' pride may ring wi' the sounds o' merry glee,
The palace ne'er was built that's frae human troubles free.

There are dreams o' the past that we wadna like to tine,
That ne'er dee in the heart, and mak' haly auld langsyne ;
When eild comes creepin' on, and life's gloaming drawin' near,
'Tis sweet to cherish thochts that are still to mem'ry dear.

We dinna mind the time when our life was in its dawn,
We drank the milk o' love, fresh frae love's warm fountain
      drawn ;
But mem'ry minds fu weel lang ere thochts gaed far aglee,
When bricht the peat fire blazed neth the big pat on the swee.

Bairns may hae hackit heels, 'rin aboot wi' broken taes,
And haughty scorn may sneer at the wee things' tattered
    claes ;
But wha can read their fate, wha can tell what they may be ?
Bricht gems are in the yirth, and dull pearls are in the sea.

What tho' in cloutit duds they gang barefit to the schule,
And mony cuffs may dree by some petty tyrant's rule ?
The wee smowts parritch-fed, wi' their rosy cheeks o' health,
May lang afore they dee be great men o' worth and wealth.

Sae, wha wad scrimp their farls, wha their luggies wad mak
    sma',
Or wha wad keep them doun gif they ettle to be braw ?
Wi' young hearts fu' o' glaiks, and their wee heids fu' o' fun,
They mak' their baws o' tow, and they fire their bourtree gun.

Some bairns to callants grow, and the carritch weel they learn,
Get heels owre heid in love ere a bawbee they can earn ;
Their hearts are in a lowe, and there's glamour in their een,
And buckled they maun get as their gutchers auld hae been.

Mean folks may siccar be, and may hain what they can spare,
And when eneugh they get, they may pant and grien for mair ;
But gear begets na peace, and, whaur comforts seem sae rife,
Hopes fade and hearts are wrung in maist ilka sphere o' life.

The mind is no' a thing that mere human art can frame,
It lifts cauld poortith up, and it tak's the gaet to fame ;

Ye wha on creepies sit may yet fill some chair o' state,
And names that aince were low may be numbered wi' the
    great.

It is a dowie hame glisks o' sunshine disna cheer,
Whaur nae kind han' o' love dichts frae sorrow's cheek the
    tear ;
The doure may yarp and girn, honest toil may save frae
    shame,
It's a' richt to hae faith, but it winna stech the wame.

Let creeds and freets abee, and shake aff a' courin fear,
The gaet that a' maun gang nane but coofs wad ever speer ;
Tak' reason for your guide, and aye keep awa frae sin,
And in the end ye may a bricht crown o' glory win.

Common Sense.

AS the guid for some end hae aft muckle to dree,
It is better, my frien', to let some things abee;
When a man is laigh doun, we sud gie him a heeze,
And aye keep the heart warm, lest our feelins sud freeze.

Let the priests rave and rant aboot brumstane and hell,
God has gien ye a mind aye to think for yoursel;
Bring your reason to bear on the straught moral line,
And ye'll see it is traced by a hand that's divine.

As our time is but short and our wants are but sma',
Sune life's sun will gang doun, and the mools cover a';
But while brichtly it shines, we sud bask in its rays,
And be couthie and guid to the end o' our days.

Fools may just as weel try to get honey frae saut
As to fin' ane on earth without some bit wee faut;
There's nae warld that we ken that is free frae a' strife,
Still, to love and be loved is the object o' life.

As the man o' soun' sense his ain worth never blaws,
Let us search for the guid, and be blin' to wee flaws ;
But tho' strong ties sud break and auld frien'ships sud part,
Tear the mask frae the loun that is hollow at heart.

Patience tholes wi' a man wi' his harns unco saft ;
Pity feels for the chiel that's catwittit and daft ;
But the whurliwha scamp wi' a tongue o' deceit
Wha wad virtue destroy sud be lashed thro' the street.

Coofs wi' siller may brag o' their ill-gotten gains,
And may sneer at the poor wi' pows stecht fu' o' brains ;
But the humble may rise, and the proud hae a fa',
Like a snaw-wreath is gowd that may sune melt awa.

Vice may weave a thick veil that may hide for a time
A' the howffs whaur her sons learn their lessons o' crime ;
She may prate o' her slaves that to fause pleasures cleave,
But, like Spunkie, she shines on life's waste to deceive.

Without siller, my frien', it is gey hard to fend,
But gif toil be yer lot, ye may win in the end ;
Tho' the gaet may be mirk that thro' life ye maun gae,
Aye keep up a licht heart while ye speel the stey brae.

To be buckled is guid gif nae taupie ye wed,
Sae be sure ye wale ane that's weelfaur'd an weel bred ;
The best blessin' o' earth is a marrow for life
Of wohm virtue feels proud as a mither and wife.

And whate'er be yer faith, and whate'er be yer creed,
Never turn a deef lug to the bairnies o' need;
Sud a' things thrive weel and nae mishaps befa'.
Ne'er forget an auld frien' when his back's at the wa'.

Ye may aiblins be rich, or may be unco poor,
But ye' canna keep Death lang awa frae yer door;
He is true to his trust, and he girns at man's gowd,
While his cauld han' o' ice rows him up in a shroud.

There's an Eye that ne'er sleeps frae whilk nae man can flee,
And a buik kept aboon that nae mortal can see;
There is due credit gien for guid deeds that we do,
So I bid ye, auld frien', for the present *adieu!*

The Wonderfu' Callant.

WI' a round bit bruckit face and tousie heid o' hair,
He thrives like a thistle wild wi' unco little care;
Tho' he's clad in cloutit duds wi' hackit hands and toes,
Sound in health wi' gustfu' air he gorbles up his brose.

The wee pawkie laddie dreams o' playmates at the schools,
O' his ba's and dozin taps and pouches fu' o' bools;
Wi' the art that bairns soon learn he gars his pearie birr,
And rins like a whittret gleg ahint a ginglin' girr.

Whaur white clouds in beauty hing ower fields o' wavin' green,
Up whaur skylarks sing their sangs his dragon may be seen;
His bit heart wi' rapture loups; the prince that wears a croun
Never feels a thrill o' joy like this wee ragged loun.

What kens he o' rackin' pains, o' fevers, and o' chills?
Puir folk ne'er hae shilpit gorbs that live on drugs and pills;
On nae feather-bed he rests, but on a laigh shakedown,
And, wi' pussie by his side, nae ane could sleep mair soun.

On his rabbits and his doos the callant kindly dauts,
And his mither's love is blin' to a' his wee bit fauts;

And to please her notions guid, and keep awa the deil,
He aft reads the buik o' Faith, and learns the carritch weel.

See him wi' his shinty club, and see him hail his ba',
Pechin hard the lave may rin, he fairly bangs them a';
Ilka thing the birkie tries he bravely bears the gree,
And, nae matter what he says, he scorns to tell a lee.

The auld notes his grannie croons he whistles and he sings :
Fond o' noise like ither bairns, his bummer round he swings :
When schule weans wad do him wrang, and he is no' to blame,
Ae lick frae his hardy nieve will send them greetin' hame.

When the snaw is on the moor, and sheep are in the fauld,
And the frosts lock up the burns, and winds blaw snell and
          cauld,
Till his rosy cheeks get blac wi' drift that blins the ee,
You can see him in the fecht whaur snawba's thickest flee.

Tho' he scarts the parritch pat, has bauchles on his feet,
Still, beneath a creeshie brat a noble heart may beat ;
What the future has in store we wisely dinna ken,
The boy-hero yet may be a hero amang men.

We ken only what he is, but no' what he may be,
What lies hidden in the brain the wisest canna see ;
But the time will come when worth, and not the chance o'
          birth,
A strong ruling power shall be and felt throughout the earth.

JOHN CENTER.

HE was taught in the Hielan's his ain mither tongue,
  And philibegs graced his teugh hurdies when young ;
When a callant, he played on the bagpipes fu' weel,
And wad carry to market a pack or a creel.

John's a pure-blooded Celt, and is nae human cur,
And will stick to a frien' firm and fast as a burr ;
When louns heartless wad crush or laws siccar oppress,
A kind lug he aye lends to the tale o' distress.

Altho' no unco buirdly, he's wiry in frame,
And for labor wad pit swankie birkies to shame ;
Ever free frae a' pride, save the pride o' a man
That will do for himsel' aye the best that he can.

Let poortith stare at him wi' a purse that is toom,
And just gie him a desert, he'll sune make it bloom ;
What cares he tho' his gear may amount na' to much,
Since maist ilka thing turns into gowd at his touch ?

He's aye busy at wark, and, as sure's ye're alive,
Like the queen-bee he'll banish the drones frae his hive ;
He can flourish whaur ithers wad perish and rot,
But for bairn-getting John micht as weel be a stot !

Wi' an eye that is keen and a head that is soun',
Ye can scarce fin' his match a' the hale kintra roun' ;
He is blest wi' strong sense, and the pawkie odd brick
Cares as little for priests as he does for auld Nick.

He still fechts wi' the courts and he fechts wi' the laws,
And he shows how the land-deeds are covered wi' flaws ;
But nae matter how cloudy John's claims may appear,
He can read thro' the darkness his ain title clear.

The great chieftain o' squatters is law-read and wise,
And frae marshes o' mud he's made beauty arise ;
Were the place only fit for puir mortals to dwell,
He wad strongly dispute the deil's title to hell !

Like the cock on the middin that craws unco crouse,
Sae auld-farrant and couthie he rules his ain house ;
Owre the nappy wi friens he is dead-sweer to part,
And a bonnie bit lass can dance aff wi' his heart.

As time dims the bricht ee and seams deep the brent brow,
So the winter o' age will soon whiten the pow ;
Wi' a conscience that's clear and an air o' content,
Oh ! may ilk ane look back at a lifetime weel spent.

THE HAPPY PAIR.

THERE'S a couthie bit body, a cantie auld cock,
  Wha is kent by the odd name o' Bob Gowenlock;
Time has mown a' the hair frae the tap o' his croun,
Yet still left him, tho' threescore an' twa, unco soun.

Idle clashes an' clavers he ne'er minds ava,
But has aye got a kind word to say aboot a';
To the wee fauts o' ithers this guid man is blind,
And a heart that is warmer wad hard be to find.

Blest wi' plenty, auld Bob is a frien' to the poor,
And the beggar in want finds relief at his door;
Wi' the best o' mankind there is aye some bit flaw,
So, if he is nae perfect, his failings are sma'.

The carl likes his drap toddy, a pinch o' guid snuff,
And whiles wi' a cuttie pipe takes a bit puff;
When cronies aboot him in festive mirth stand,
He will sing the auld sangs o' his ain native land.

He is blest wi' a leal and a kind-hearted wife,
Wha has shared a' his cares thro' the maist o' his life ;
Oh ! the sweet, hinnied words that fa' saft frae her tongue
Cast around him love's sunshine as when they were young.

The guid Buik frae whase pages the blind seek for licht
The auld pair read a portion o't mornin' and nicht ;
As they feel that life's blessings a' come frae above,
So their hame is the hame o' contentment and love.

A' Bob's riches were gained by the sweat o' his brow,
And when toiling for age he was happy as now ;
Aye content wi' the sphere where his lot was lang cast,
He delights wi' his friens yet to crack o' the past.

Things are never sae pure that there's nae room to mend,
And the frugal will aye fin' oot some way to fend ;
In the springtime provide for the autumn o' life,
And wale weel aboon a' things. a trusty, guid-wife.

Jamie McGinn,

A COMICAL UNDERTAKER OF SAN FRANCISCO.

HERE sleeps my old friend, Irish Jamie McGinn,
  Who gave up the ghost with a comical grin ;
He thought all the rogues would be left in the lurch
Who put not their faith in the old Mother Church ;
Of gin he was fond, and could relish a feast,
And count his round beads with the grace of a priest.
For long years before Jamie's own spirit fled,
He laughed with the living, and buried the dead ;
At the half-way house known as Purgatory,
He was rubbed and scrubbed and made fit for glory ;
Yea, even the stain of original sin
Was washed from the hide of saint Jamie McGinn.

LINES

WRITTEN THE NIGHT BEFORE I LEFT CALIFORNIA, OCTOBER 17, 1870.

I WILL remember till life's close
  A few friends warm and kind :
But little else I have to leave
  Save buried hopes behind.

———•◆•———

LINES

WRITTEN THE MORNING OF LEAVING CALIFORNIA.

FAREWELL, my friends ! a long farewell,
  To each and all a fond adieu !
Within my breast a grateful heart
  Through life shall ne'er turn cold to you.

———•◆•———

AFFINITY AND DIVINITY.

AS chemists never doubt the truth
  Of physical affinity,
So goodness magnet-like draws man
  The nearer to Divinity.

9

SONGS.

I Feel I'm Growing Auld, Gude-wife.

I FEEL I'm growing auld, gude-wife—
　　I feel I'm growing auld ;
My steps are frail, my een are bleared,
　　My pow is unco bauld.
I've seen the snaws o' fourscore years
　　O'er hill and meadow fa',
And, hinnie ! were it no for you,
　　I'd gladly slip awa'.

I feel I'm growing auld, gude-wife—
　　I feel I'm growing auld ;
Frae youth to age I've keepit warm
　　The love that ne'er turned cauld.
I canna bear the dreary thocht
　　That we maun sindered be ;
There's naething binds my poor auld heart
　　To earth, gude-wife, but thee.

I feel I'm growing auld, gude-wife—
　　I feel I'm growing auld ;

Life seems to me a wintry waste,
  The very sun feels cauld.
Of worldly friens ye've been to me
  Amang them a' the best;
Now I'll lay down my weary head,
  Gude-wife, and be at rest.

TAK' BACK THE RING, DEAR JAMIE.

TAK' back the ring, dear Jamie,
  The ring ye gae to me,
An' a' the vows ye made yestreen
  Beneath the birken-tree.
But gie me back my heart again,
  It's a' I hae to gie ;
Sin' ye'll no wait a fittin' time,
  Ye canna marry me.

I promised to my daddie,
  Afore he slipp'd awa,
I ne'er wad leave my minnie,
  Whate'er sud her befa'
I'll faithfu' keep my promise,
  For a' that ye can gie :
Sae, Jamie, gif ye winna wait,
  Ye ne'er can marry me.

I canna leave my minnie,
  She's been sae kind to me

Sin' e'er I was a bairnie,
  A wee thing on her knee.
Nae mair she'll caim my gowden hair,
  Nor busk me snod an' braw;
She's auld an' frail, her een are dim,
  An' sune will close on a'.

I maunna leave my minnie,
  Her journey is na lang;
Her heid is bendin' to the mools,
  Where it maun shortly gang.
'Were I an heiress o' a crown,
  I'd a' its honors tine,
'To watch her steps in helpless age,
  As she in youth watched mine.

THE SNAW LIES DEEP ON HILL AND PLAIN.

THE snaw lies deep on hill and plain,
  Snell fa' the pelting sleet and rain ;
Sure winter has come back again,
    Wi' nichts baith lang and wearie O ;
The Sun's withdrawn his cheering beams,
The ice has fettered living streams,
And a' the face o' Nature seems
    A desert cauld and drearie O.

O'er earth a spotless robe is flung,
Wi' white festoons the groves are hung,
Whaur sylvan minstrels lately sung
    Their touching lays sae cheerie O ;
There's frost-work on the window-pane,
And flocks for green fields bleat in vain ;
Sure winter has come back again,
    And winds blaw wild and eerie O.

But what care I for whistling winds,
Or drifting snaw that fairly blinds ?
Gie me the joys that true love finds
    Beside my trusting dearie O.

Sae fondly still to me she clings,
And sunshine o'er life's pathway flings,
Wi' music sweet our cottage rings,
    That mak's our hame sae cheerie O.

KATE O' GLENROWAN.

AT the auld parish kirk sin' I was a callant,
　Fair lassies I've seen that were winsome and braw :
But for beauty o' grace and a bonnie sweet face,
　The charmin' young Kate is the flower o' them a'.

She's fair as the white-rose, and pure as the snow-flakes;
　Her tender heart beats sae confidin' and true,
And were Kate only mine, with a transport divine
　I'd bask in the light o' her twa een o' blue.

But, oh! what gars me dream o' Kate, the rich heiress,
　Or cherish a hope that is foolish and vain ?
While I love her blindly, she smiles on me kindly,
　And not with proud looks of a haughty disdain.

As her daddie's a laird, she rides in her carriage,
　And flunkies braw-drest on their young mistress wait ;
The auld folks caress her, the beggars a' bless her,
　And ilk ane is loud in the praises o' Kate.

Oh ! were Kate only puir, without lands or siller,
 To open her heart love wad sune find a key ;
But had I ne'er met her, or could I forget her,
 I'd then be as blest as a bodie can be.

Over hopes that are crushed I feel dull and dowie,
 And nae ane can tell what I silently dree ;
The days are sae drearie, the nichts lang and wearie,
 There's naething noo left to bring comfort to me.

My Mary O.

I WAD na gie my Mary yet
  For a' the lassies I hae seen;
Upon her face twa roses bloom,
  And love shines in her bonnie een.
She sings as sweet as ony bird—
  Like some wee witching fairy O ;
She's crept into this heart o' mine,
  And there she reigns my Mary O.

Blest wi' a heart that's pure and true,
  And wi' a form that's grace itsel',
Does mortal breathe wha could na feel
  The charming power o' sic a spell ?
Queen o' my love ! I vow to thee
  That while on earth I tarry O,
No one shall share this heart o' mine
  Wi' my sweet, winsome Mary O.

CLARA.

SWEET as a lyre by angel strung
  Flows gushing music from her tongue;
And in her warm, confiding heart
Love plays its true and gentle part.
In her all human virtues blend
That gild life's pathway to the end;
With witching grace she smiles on all,
And lends an ear to Pity's call.

Seam not her brow, O plowman Care!
Such beauty sweet in mercy spare;
Through weary life, so sad and brief,
Wring not her heart, O weeping Grief!
The smiles upon her bonnie face,
And all her charms of winning grace,
Stamp Clara such a peerless prize
Might lure an angel from the skies.

Annie Lee.

—————

HOW sweet 'tis to think o' lang syne, Annie Lee !
  When youth, grace, and beauty were thine, Annie Lee!
      When heart beat against heart
        Whaur nae ane could see,
     I thocht thee an angel
       O' bliss, Annie Lee !

Ere Nature had taught us to lo'e, Annie Lee !
'Mang clover-fields wet wi' the dew, Annie Lee !
      We'd list to the skylark
        That sprang frae the lee ;
     But sweeter by far were
       Thy songs, Annie Lee !

Down the glen we aft took a turn, Annie Lee !
An' laved our wee feet in the burn, Annie Lee !
      I looked at thy shadow,
        An' then upon thee,
     An' felt as if spell-bound
       To love, Annie Lee!

Wi' bonnie rich ringlets o' hair, Annie Lee!
I never sae ane look sae fair, Annie Lee!
 An' thy twa een o' blue,
  That sparkled wi' glee,
 Never shone to deceive
  My heart, Annie Lee!

1 thocht earth a heaven o' bliss, Annie Lee!
When young courage stole the first kiss, Annie Lee!
 The flowers were nae fairer
  That bloom on the lea,
 The snawdraps nae purer
  Than thou, Annie Lee!

The pure heart that's free frae a' sin, Annie Lee!
In the end is aye sure to win, Annie Lee!
 So, we ne'er dreamt o' wrang;
  Oh! wha wad wrang thee?
 Sweet mate o' my boyhood,
  My dear Annie Lee!

Aft love gets what gold canna buy, Annie Lee!
An' gif ony doot, let them try, Annie Lee!
 They will find to their grief
  That a' their hopes dee,
 And naething but love lives
  In bliss, Annie Lee!

It is said that true love is blind, Annie Lee!
An' seldom a leal heart can find, Annie Lee!

But the flame waneth not
  First kindled by thee ;
'Tis fanned by thy love still,
  My sweet Annie Lee !

LITTLE NELLY GORDON.

SWEET little Nelly Gordon,
  So witching and so airy,
Thy step is like the gentle fawn,
  Or some wee mountain fairy.

Young rosebud of Life's joyous Spring,
  Where pride and hope are centred,
Thine eyes are love, thy heart a shrine
  Where sin has never entered.

Sweet little Nelly Gordon !
  Fair bud that soon will blossom,
May sorrow never plant her thorns
  Within thy tender bosom.

If on this orb, sweet, beauteous thing,
  Thou art designed to tarry,
Seek till thou find the jewel, worth,
  And not till then e'er marry.

MY BONNIE WEE LIZZIE.

MY bonnie wee Lizzie,
  So gentle and fair,
There's love in thy glances,
  And grace in thine air.
My heart, like the ivy
  That twines round the tree,
Clings fondly with rapture,
  My Lizzie, to thee.

Sweet flower of rare beauty,
  My hope and my pride !
I never feel happy
  Away from thy side.
May no clouds of sorrow
  E'er shade thy young brow,
Nor tears bleach the roses
  That sweetly bloom now.

Thine eyes beam so brightly
  And softly on me,

No wonder that nightly
  My dreams are of thee.
I'll go to the altar
  With joy and with pride,
And there, my sweet Lizzie,
  Confess thee my bride.

My Sweet Little Hinnie.

"MY sweet little Hinnie,
  My bonnie wee doo!
What sets me a-dreaming
  An' thinking o' you?
The sly, pawkie archer
  Has wounded my heart.
And none but you, Mary,
  Can pluck out the dart."

" Gif that be sae, Willy,
  I'll pluck out the dart.
And I'll gie you mysel'
  To heal your bit heart.
I'll be your leal wifie
  E'en sud I repent;
So aff to my minnie,
  And spier her consent."

" I'll aff, my wee dantee—
  Ae kiss ere I gang;

The lift it is starry,
  The road is na lang.
I'll sune be back, lassie,
  Love's wings quickly flee ;
Then, then shall I never
  Part, Mary, frae thee."

THE VALLEY OF WYOMING.

SHOULD you resolve in happy mood
    Awhile to go a-roaming,
Rest not until your eyes behold
    The Valley of Wyoming.
Although with evening dew there falls
    No life-sustaining manna,
There Plenty spreads her ample stores
    Along the Susquehanna

The fields send forth their golden grain
    In no mean, stinted measure,
And Earth to toil yields freely up
    Her subterranean treasure.
Let poets sing the praises of
    The dashing Lackawanna ;
But give to me that noble stream,
    The charming Susquehanna.

Its fertile banks are sweetly graced
    By many a cot and palace,

And hills of green look proudly down
  Upon the peaceful valleys.
There blooms the rosebud of my heart,
  The young and peerless Anna;
No purer is thy crystal stream,
  O placid Susquehanna!

First Love.

THO' the false world may hide, and sly art may conceal,
  There is no love so pure as the first love we feel ;
While we try to supplant it or tear it apart,
Like a sweet, clasping vine it clings close to the heart.

On the ruins of some broken heart it may lean,
And grow like wild weeds in the ocean unseen ;
While roses of beauty may languish and fade,
Like some tender exotic that's kept in the shade.

The sweet smiles of a face and bright, love-speaking eyes
For a season the passion may partly disguise ;
And the heart may be sad while the tongue may be still,
Yet it lives warmly nursed, let us do what we will.

To remembrance it clings, and it clings to the soul,
And to banish it thence baffles human control ;
It is true to its object of love and of worth,
As the mariner's needle that points to the north.

12

Just as well strive to flee from the presence of God
As to pluck out the passion, at home or abroad;
It is nourished with sighs, it is watered with tears,
And how bitter and dark is the fruit that it bears!

Like some flower of rare beauty whose delicate form
Is too fragile to brave the rude blasts of life's storm;
Oh! for pity's sake spare it from slander's foul breath,
Till its beatings are hushed in the stillness of death.

Mary Ann,

OF HAMILTON, ONTARIO.

I'VE wandered ower this weary warld,
  And seen some beauties rare ;
But till I met sweet Mary Ann,
  I ne'er saw ane sae fair.

Her wee bit heart is love itsel,
  And her twa witchin' een
Need not the music o' her tongue
  To tell me what they mean.

Nae beauty that I ever saw
  Can match her winsome face ;
And, cast in nature's fairest mould,
  Her form is perfect grace.

So, love, bring all your charming queens
  That sweetly smile on man ;
There's ane I ken will beat them a'—
  My bonnie Mary Ann.

Lucy Lee.

———

SHE'S budding in her early teens,
  Sae young and sweetly fair;
What hand wad in her bosom plant
  The thorns o' grief an' care?
The mother on her bairnie doats
  That smiles upon her knee;
But wi' a warmer gush o' joy
  My heart lo'es Lucy Lee.

There's love in a' her witching smiles,
  There's rapture in her een;
I need no aid o' mystic lore
  To tell me what they mean.
The warld and a' that in it blooms
  Wad be a waste to me,
Did frosts untimely nip the flower,
  My winsome Lucy Lee.

Have You Felt at Your Heart?

HAVE you felt at your heart
   The strong tuggings of sin,
When the flame of pure love
   Was first kindled within?
Have you sworn to be true,
   In soft whispers sincere,
When heart beat against heart,
   And when no one is near?

Have you knelt to blue eyes
   As you would at a shrine,
Without feeling the wish
   That the fair one was thine?
Have you tasted the sweets
   Of a maiden's first kiss,
Without thinking you breathed
   In a region of bliss?

If you have, then away
   With your cold heart of stone,

And in some desert dwell,
Like a hermit, alone.
Let me bask in the smiles
Of the fond one I love,
Till my soul, tired of earth,
Seeks a blest home above.

I Love to Dream o' Thee, Mary!

WHEN Nature tak's her winter nap
   In her cauld white sheets o' snaw,
Or when the wild, weird whistlin' winds
   Roun' the auld clay biggin blaw,
An' meltin' rains an roarin' floods
   A' the strong ice-fetters thaw,
How I love to dream o' thee, Mary!
   How I love to dream o' thee!

When tender shoots an' burstin' buds
   On the orchard trees are hung;
When wee birds build their cosie nests,
   Whaur the auld anes feed their young,
An' hills an' valleys ring wi' joy,
   As they aft before hae rung,
How I love to dream o' thee, Mary!
   How I love to dream o' thee!

When the thorn is white wi' blossoms,
   An' the bloom is on the pea;

When bonnie golden buttercups
  An' the gowans gem the lee,
An' kindred tribes in sylvan groves
  Sing on ilka bush an' tree,
How I love to dream o' thee, Mary!
  How I love to dream o' thee!

When bleatin' hills an' vocal glens
  Lie bathed in glittering sheen,
Ere gloamin' casts a dusky veil
  O'er the fields o' wavin' green,
Or lovers meet to pledge their vows
  At the trystin' time o' e'en,
How I love to dream o' thee, Mary!
  How I love to dream o' thee!

When the flowers a' droop an' wither,
  Despite the dews that gently fa';
When the yellow hairsts are gathered in,
  An' the swallows flee awa';
When the nichts are lang an' dreary,
  An' a gloom hangs over a',
How I love to dream o' thee, Mary!
  How I love to dream o' thee!

LOWLAND MARY.

THE rosy rays of the morning light
   In their downward course may tarry
And linger to gild the mountain-tops,
   Ere I cease to love my Mary.
The rolling spheres may be lost in night,
   The sun in his course may vary;
But my constant heart will aye beat true
   To my own dear Lowland Mary.

O'er my head the clouds of care may hang,
   And my cherished hopes miscarry;
But no changes that the world may bring
   Can e'er change my love for Mary;
Trees may not bloom, and birds may not sing,
   And the speed of time may vary;
But warmly throned in this loving heart
   Shall reign my own Lowland Mary.

How the Heart to the Past wi' Rapture Clings !

HOW the heart to the Past wi' rapture clings
　　When the spirit Memory bears nae stings,
But o'er it a glorious halo flings
　　That makes it seem sae cheerie !
There's a bonnie wee spot ayont the sea
That's sweeter than a' ither spots to me,
Where the mornin' o' life I spent sae free
　　'Mang scenes that never wearie.

There the Spring first comes wi' its leaves and buds ;
There the cuckoo is heard in the circlin' wuds ;
An' far up in the lift amang the cluds
　　The laverock sings sae cheerie.
The swallow its wings in the burnie dips ;
The bee frae the thistle its honey sips ;
Where sae fondly first I pried the lips
　　O' Jean, my bonnie dearie.

Oh! my heart yet clings, Craigieburn, to thee!
Where the langest day was aye short to me;
An' where aften I still in fancy flee
    To scenes that never wearie.
I dream o' the trees wi' their plumes o' green,
An' I gaze on the flowers wi' ravished een,
Where first I met wi' my bonnie Jean,
    My early, only dearie.

JESSIE PATERSON.

WHERE green hills gently rise, and the Tweed is but
    a burn,
In pleasing dreams of fancy my footsteps oft return ;
But sic happy days again I never mair may see ;
Oh ! then Jessie Paterson was a' the world to me.

Red rowans an' blae-berries in simmer we wad pu',
An' wi' licht hearts, free o' care, we promised to be true ;
But how little do we ken what we're born to dree and
    tine ?
Then a' her hopes an' prospects were bundled up wi'
    mine.

Oh ! Blink-Bonny's buddin' rose was fairest o' the fair,
An' gracefully in ringlets hung down her gowden hair ;
We never thocht o' changes the future had in store,
Or the pangs that it wad bring we dreamt-na o' before.

When her wee cozie biggin, weel theekit ower wi' straw,
Wi' Winter's robe was happit, afore March brocht a thaw ;

Or when flowers wad bud in Spring, and braird was on
    the lea,
Oh! then Jessie Paterson was a' the world to me.

When the sun in mornin' mist was blinkin' redly through,
An' the gowan an' the broom were bricht wi' pearly dew,
We've listened to the lark in some fleecy-flittin' cloud,
Where sweet the little warbler sung matin lays aloud.

In the merry harvest-time, when reapers cam' to shear,
We thocht-na in our daffin' our partin' was so near;
I think I see her now, fu' o' rosy, rustic glee;
Oh! then Jessie Paterson was a' the world to me.

But why should I be dowie? Thae days are gane an' past,
An' I hae learned the lesson that pleasures canna last;
Her minnie was-na pleased, an' anger steek'd the door;
The truth then stood revealed that I was unco poor.

Bonnie Jessie Paterson! sae winsome an' sae kind,
Keep a wee neuk in your heart for honest Tam the hind;
Though Willie ye hae wed, an' crossed the heavin' sea,
My blessin' on ye baith—lang happy may ye be!

OH! MY FAIR, MY DARLING MAGGIE.

OH! my fair, my darling Maggie,
 Angel, whom I love so dearly;
Language fails to speak the feeling
 Of my heart, that beats sincerely.

Chorus—Let us live to love each other,
  Bound by ties that none can sever;
 Now, my fair, my darling Maggie,
  Say thou wilt be mine for ever.

Love from life's warm fountain gushes;
 Kisses tell what ne'er was spoken;
Vows are but poor empty pledges,
 Warmly made and coldly broken.
Chorus—Let us live to love each other, etc.

Gliding down life's rapid river,
 We can hear the wild birds singing;
They may teach us to be happy—
 Fondly to their spring mates clinging.
Chorus—Let us live to love each other, etc.

Bonnie Fanny Dean.

IN rambling through this weary warld,
　I've flowers o' beauty seen ;
But nane were half sae fair to me
　As bonnie Fanny Dean.

I've never seen sic twa blue een,
　Nor sic a sweet wee mou ;
And, oh ! her heart is soft and pure
　As drops o' morning dew.

The glossy vine wi' grace may twine
　In nature's wilds amang ;
More gracefu' still ower Fanny's brow
　Her gowden tresses hang.

I've kent her sin' she was a bairn,
　A wee bit gentle thing ;
But never thocht her budding charms
　A spell wad ower me fling.

I'll never break the sacred vow,
The promise made yestreen;
Come weal or woe, I'll wedded be
To bonnie Fanny Dean.

EPITAPHS AND EPIGRAMS.

SANDY MIEN.

MIEN by name and mean by nature,
  Mean in looks and mean in stature,
Mean in line and every feature,
Lived this mean and worthless creature.

ON THE TOMBSTONE OF A KNAVE.

AS from death there is no one exempt,
  Here lie the remains of a knave,
For whose name, just to show their contempt
  Skunks come here and water his grave.

AN HONEST MAN.

PAUSE, reader, for a moment pause,
　　And shed one silent tear;
For, underneath this lonely mound,
　　An honest man sleeps here.

———▸◆◂———

ELLIS THE BAKER.

HERE lies the sot, Ellis the baker,
　　Who, when living, was selfish and cold;
For some unaccountable reason,
　　Mercy spared him until he was old.

———▸◆◂———

THE DRUNKARD AND CHEAT.

HERE lies an impostor, a drunkard and cheat,
　　Whom the rogues called the prince of guid fellows;
He tried to cheat Death, but he did not succeed,
　　Yet succeeded in cheating the gallows.

THE HYPOCRITE.

THIS man tried his best to serve God and the Devil,
　　But he loved most of all his hot toddy;
A wild, fevered brain made a wreck of his soul,
　　And the whisky a hell of his body.

LYING TOMMY.

IF truth he speaks, 'tis by mistake,
　　And none but fools believe him;
When old grim Death chokes Tommy's breath,
　　The Devil will receive him.

DRAM-DRINKING JOHN.

HE drank so much brandy while living
　　That the chemists all said he would keep
Till the angel shall blow the last trump,
　　When amazed he will start from his sleep.

On the Death of a Friend.

AND couldst thou not, O cruel Death !
　　Withheld the fatal blow
That so untimely laid my friend
　　And dear companion low ?

————•◆•————

On the Death of Robert Gowanlock,

OF SAN FRANCISCO.

SO thou art gone, O good old man !
　　My long-tried friend and brother !
How vain the search would be on earth
　　To find just such another !

————•◆•————

Epigram.

HIS heart is as rotten as muck,
　　And black as the color of coal ;
Inquiry dumbfounded was struck
　　In finding no trace of a soul.

Elder Knapp, the Sensational Preacher.

FOR God's sake and your own sake, Knapp,
　　Don't preach such silly twaddle,
But leave this fair Pacific coast,
　　And to the East skedaddle !

———→•←———

The Ruling Passion.

HE raved and he swore, and he hobbled about,
　　To brandy a slave, and a martyr to gout;
Though not bent with years, he was long spared to see
His finger-joints gnarled like the trunk of a tree;
While tortured with pangs from his head to his toes,
The blossoms of rum flourished red on his nose;
Like one that was bent in the search of more pain,
He freely would drink Widow Clicquot champagne;
He died as he lived, and, while gasping for breath,
His last grog was quaffed in the Valley of Death.

DAVID MITCHELL.

THERE'S Mitchell, he treasures up learning,
  But cares not for hoarding up pelf;
He has but one foe in the world,
  And, strange to say, that is himself.
Some say that he likes pretty girls,
  And hint that he's fond of his toddy;
It may be all true, but I swear
  His heart is too big for his body.

WILLY, THE ANTIQUARIAN ODDITY.

MADE up of strange and *outre* parts,
  Oh! queer, incongruous mixture,
You crept into my heart langsyne,
  And there remained a fixture.
There's something about thee, old friend!
  So lively and so active,
That makes thy humor and thy wit
  So sparkling and attractive.

EPIGRAM.

WHILE e'en the very best may be
    A little indiscreet,
There's nothing in the wrangler, but
    The gas of self-conceit.